Letter to Santa

By

Racquel Henry

Marabella House Books

Viola

Viola held the sapphire ring in the palm of her hand and stared at it. She closed her palm and let the weight of metal and stone sink into her skin. It was as heavy as her heart. She should be over this by now.

It had been ten long months since she ended things with Mark Winston—ten long months since she had a clear enough head to illustrate or design anything. On paper, he was perfect. He was charming, smart, and kind. He had the recently acquired job that provided stable income, the new house, the car—all the right threads that would sew their dream life together. They were right out of college, and they were both on a fast track. When he proposed, she thought she'd spend the rest of her life with him, lazing around the house on Sunday mornings, on his arm when they attended the future weddings of friends, and watching sunsets from their back porch. Once they tied the knot, Viola would work on getting her greeting card business off the ground.

The timer on the toaster oven signaled her toast was done. She trudged to the kitchen and poured herself a cup of coffee. She had to figure out a way to get herself out of this messy state. She was certain she wouldn't last much longer if she kept it up. The problem was that she had tried to pick up her pieces so many times before. The latest thing was meditation, and self-care, and self-love, and self-acceptance. Self, self, self. At her core, she loved herself, but she didn't need everyone shoving it down her throat every two seconds. What about just taking the necessary time to heal?

She glanced at the time on the stove. In twenty-two minutes, she had to be at the adoption center where she worked to write letters to Santa with the children. When her dear friend, Mrs. Walker, had told her about the job a few months ago, she felt an instant need to lend a hand. After losing her own parents in an accident when she was sixteen, she knew what it was like to feel alone. Some of the counselors thought it would be nice to give them the best Christmas experience possible. That meant letters to Santa, regardless of who still believed in him.

Though it had been a rough morning of traipsing down memory lane, she had to admit she was looking forward to it. Making a difference for the kids was actually making a difference for her too. She wanted to hold on to that as long as she could. She had even told the counselors that she'd give as much of her time as she could beyond her regular work hours. She finished eating her toast, gulped the rest of her pumpkin spiced coffee, and slipped into her favorite glittery holiday sweater.

The air was crisp in Central Florida as she stepped out of the door of her apartment building. Despite her moping around this morning, the cool air and the spirit of the Christmas season dancing through it made her hopeful. Christmas was her favorite holiday, and she wasn't going to let anyone ruin it for her. Just as she rounded the corner to the parking lot, she bumped into a rock, hard… chest?

"Ouch," she said, rubbing her forehead.

"Excuse me. I didn't see you there," the voice that came with the firm body said. His voice was cavernous but gentle at the same time.

"That's because you weren't watching where you were going, and you came barreling through," she mumbled, dusting herself off.

"I was in a rush—I'm sorry," the guy said.

She was just about to make another smart comment when she glanced up and saw two sets of the most mesmerizing brown eyes she had ever seen. They had tiny droplets of gold speckled in them like they were designed specifically for hypnotizing. She couldn't remember where she was, what time of day it was, or where she was going. She tried to blink, but her eyes remained resistant.

"Are you okay?" the guy said, narrowing his eyes.

Viola heard his voice, but couldn't comprehend what he was saying.

He gave her an awkward smile, and she finally broke out of the trance.

"Just be careful where you're going, next time. Other people live in this building too, you know." She couldn't hide the irritation in her voice if she tried. The cold air had lifted her spirit for a second and now here was this gorgeous, tall, interruption with a concrete chest crashing right into her—killing the high. She took a deep breath and realized the thought that just ran through her head. She was complaining because a hot guy bumped into her? She frowned.

"Are you sure you're okay?" he asked again.

His eyes transfixed her again, and this time a flutter grazed over her heart. What must she have looked like as her nutty thoughts took over? "I'm fine," she said, lowering her voice a level to try and take some of the edge out of it.

"Sorry again," he said, taking his time to move away.

She sighed. She had to work harder at not letting her past affect her present. She shouldn't take out her bitterness for Mark on other people. Calling off her engagement was the best gift Mark could have given her. They were never right for each other, and she knew it. The problem was, if she knew they were going nowhere, why did it still sting so much?

Charlie

Charlie shook his head as he made his way to the double doors at the front of the building. That was a strange encounter. The woman he bumped into was beautiful, and right as she bumped into him, he caught the scent of lavender and coconut, which was no doubt from her curly brown hair being so close. There was a subtle rise in his chest, but he dismissed it as he dealt with the aftermath of her crashing straight into him. He reflected on the weird pauses. It was like she was having a conversation in her head instead of with him. He was guilty that he wasn't watching where he was going and that he had indeed slammed into her pretty hard. He hoped she was okay, which is why he kept asking. He'd feel terrible if he hurt her, especially since he didn't even know why he was rushing. Maybe he was just on edge from the long drive from New York. Moving across several states had taken its toll on him.

Every now and then, a memory of Holly would surface in his mind. He was glad his job took him away from the big city. He didn't hesitate when they asked him if he would consider a transfer. New York was a large enough city that he probably wouldn't run into her, but so many things in that city reminded him of her. She was at Times Square, his favorite pizza place, Grimaldi's, tangled up in the fabric of the furniture, and all the walls of his apartment.

He opened the double doors to the new apartment building and let out a deep breath. Change was good. He followed the signs to the leasing office where an older lady with curly gray hair sat at a desk. A string of colorful lights lined the perimeter of the ceiling, matching the colors on the Christmas sweater she wore. She almost jumped out of her chair when Charlie walked in.

"Sorry, I didn't mean to startle you," Charlie said.

"No, No, it's totally fine. That's what

I get for falling asleep on the job." She chuckled. "What can I do for you?"

Her chuckle was contagious, and Charlie couldn't help but join in. "My name's Charlie Palmer. I was the one who called to ask a bunch of questions and ended up reserving online," he said, beaming.

She kept her same blank expression and blinked a few times.

What was with this town and everyone's odd staring contests? He'd received more blank stares in the last ten minutes than his whole life. He cleared his throat, and she finally moved.

She shuffled through a few folders on her desk. "What was the last name again? Palmer?" she asked, looking him in the eyes for the first time, at least that's what he assumed. She had on dark sunglasses that screamed night rider.

"That's right. Palmer."

She had a distant look on her face.

"Everything alright?"

"Yeah, I just lost my marbles for a sec," she said.

Charlie laughed. She did not.

Southern hospitality be damned when

you're frustrated, he thought.

She continued to shuffle papers and folders on her desk until she said, "Aha! I knew I wasn't nuts. I had your file on my desk earlier this morning," she said, waving a blue file folder in the air. She opened it. "Okay, yeah, I can confirm you did indeed pay online to reserve your space. We still need to fill out the paperwork, though," she said. She handed him a small stack of papers.

"I thought I already did all this?" he asked.

"You wanna work at this desk and make the rules?" she said, shaking her head.

Charlie wrinkled his brow and scratched his head.

The woman breathed in as far as she could and then let the breath out. She made a dramatic show of rolling her eyes. "This is the way things are done. I like cold, hard, copies—written by hand. None of that cloud stuff. I don't trust it. You new ones are always asking too many questions," she said. She didn't say another word but instead pointed to the empty table in the corner. It was set up like a dining table he imagined to make the office seem more like home.

He felt a little off-put, but something told him not to push her envelope too far. Instead, he took his seat as instructed. He hated filling out applications of any kind. The process itself was so monotonous, which is why he had filled out one online. He thought that would be it.

He studied the page, and out of nowhere, another memory of Holly surfaced in his mind. He wondered if this was the way it was going to be from now on. Would memories of her always torture him, or would they eventually fade away? He wanted desperately to be able to control his own mind. He still cared about her, but in the five months they'd been broken up, he had drawn the conclusion they weren't a good fit. He knew it, and yet he still couldn't quite get over her fully.

He picked up the pen and sighed. As he filled out all the basic information on the application page, he relaxed. Though he hated the monotonous part of filling out the application, the process felt like a fresh start. He glanced up at the leasing office agent. She was watching the large screen on the wall in front of her desk. It was on the Hallmark channel. He shook his head and thought about how much his grandmother loved the channel. That's who this woman reminded him of, minus the spunk.

The woman glanced at him and scowled. He shouldn't have the urge to smile, but he did. This change of pace would be good for him.

Viola

After deciding to treat herself to a coffee, Viola pulled into a parking spot at the front of The Center and went inside. The Center didn't have a ton of money for decorations, so it wasn't very festive at all. She made a mental note to think of something to fix that. Maybe she could find some extra freelance design work to help pay for it.

"Hey, Viola," a pleasant voice said. Mary, one of the event coordinators, stood in the hallway that led to the activity room.

"Hi," Viola said, taking a sip of her coffee. She already felt much better just by walking through the door. The work they did here was so important. She was grateful to be a part of it. No matter what crappy things went on in her life, she was always happy here. "Mary, what do you think about a few more decorations for in here?

I'm sure the kids would love that, might even make it seem a little more like home," she said.

"I'd love that—all of us would. But the budget just doesn't allow it. We need to work on fundraising, but the volunteers and staff we have are already stretched so thin," Mary said, her voice down a few octaves. She tucked her long blonde hair behind her ear.

"I hear you. I could spend some time looking for grants and brainstorming other fundraising opportunities if you all want."

"That would be great! I just want us to do everything we can for these kids," she said.

Viola smiled. "Me too."

Mary paused for a second, then said, "But maybe don't spend too much time on it. You've given us so much, and if you ever want to get that greeting card business off the ground, you have to spend time on that too," she said.

"I know, I know. The card business can wait. These kids are important to me too. And right now, I'm getting the best of both worlds: Freelancing illustrations and helping out here," Viola said.

Mary gave Viola's shoulder a gentle squeeze. "We're lucky to have you. You ready to write to Santa?" Mary asked, clapping her hands together.

"Let's do it," Viola said as they walked down the dark, narrow hallway. The building was already an older one as it was. Some extra lights alone would go a long way to liven things up for the kids.

The activity room was noisy, but most of the kids were seated around a giant table made from several smaller ones pushed together.

"Viola! Come sit with me," a girl named Lang said.

Mary leaned over and whispered, "We're having them pair up with staff or a volunteer."

"Sounds good," Viola said, stretching her neck to see if there was an empty seat next to Lang.

"You look really pretty today," Lang said as Viola sat down.

Viola certainly didn't feel pretty, not after the pity party she had this morning. "Thank you, Lang." She turned on her brightest smile. Thinking about her morning prompted an image of the stranger she bumped into. She shook it away. He had already taken up too much space in her brain. She had a job to do right now.

"No problem. What do you think about writing these letters to Santa?" Lang asked, brushing her dark brown bangs out of her eyes.

"I think it's a great idea!" Viola said. She could use the distraction. Even though she hadn't written a letter to Santa since she was a kid, the idea of doing it again sounded like fun. It reminded her of a more simple time, a time when she still believed in Christmas magic. When had she stopped?

"Even if we're too old to believe in Santa?" Lang asked.

"When are you too old to believe in Santa?" Viola said.

"I don't know. But I'm twelve. I'm old enough to know Santa doesn't exist," Lang said.

"You're never too old to believe in Santa." Viola patted Lang's shoulder.

Lang dropped her eyes and thought for

a moment. "Hmm. If that's true, then do you believe in Santa?" she asked.

Always a tricky question, but deep down, Viola believed in Christmas magic. There may not be one specific man flying through the night sky on a sleigh, but there were such things as Christmas miracles. "I do."

"So you're going to write a letter to Santa today too, right?" Lang crossed her arms over her chest and drilled her eyes into Viola. She was one tough cookie.

"Of course I am," Viola said. What was the harm? It would be just like all those woo woo self-care people said about putting things out into the universe. She might as well let her wishes be known.

"What will you ask Santa for?" Lang asked.

She sure was full of questions. Viola could think of a few things she'd like Santa to bring her, things he most likely wasn't able to. She thought about bending the truth, but Lang was too smart for that.

"Come on, I can see on your face something popped up," Lang pressed.

"You are very perceptive," Viola said.

Lang nodded.

Cocky too, Viola thought.

"I would ask Santa for a less restless mind and my soul mate." The minute the words left Viola's lips, she wished she could take them back. She didn't really want to say it out loud.

"That's sweet," Lang said, her expression shifting from interrogative to gentle. "You should put that in your letter. Tell him that exact thing. You never know," she said in a sing-song voice.

"Hey, isn't that supposed to be my line?" Viola said, laughing.

"I learn from the best," Lang said.

Viola bumped Lang's shoulder with her own and reached for a marker. Once again, being in this place had brought her immense joy. Maybe Lang was right—there could be something to writing a letter to Santa. Just a moment ago she wondered when she lost her belief in holiday magic. Maybe this was the start to bringing it back.

Charlie

It was getting pretty late in the afternoon when Charlie realized he hadn't eaten lunch. He glanced at the time on his phone and groaned. After spending hours in the leasing office filling out paperwork, he finally had the keys to his new apartment. He had spent a little time on his phone catching up on work emails and now stood in the middle of the living room, contemplating his next move. The movers and his pod had also arrived while he worked, but he was too tired to start unpacking. He couldn't quite make something to eat either since he had no groceries. He held up his phone and said, "Restaurants near me."

"Okay, here is what I found," the phone responded.

There was a lot that came up, but he had no idea if they were any good. Reviews online can be so fickle. Why did he move to a city where he didn't know anyone? He took his time going over the list and finally settled on a taco place called Tako Cheena. It would be pretty hard to mess up tacos. On his way out, he caught a glimpse of Ms. Walker through the doors to the leasing office. She was still at her desk, only this time she was reclined, her eyes glued to the TV above. Charlie laughed as he reflected on the fact that she was still watching Christmas movies.

Outside, the air was more brisk than it was earlier. He had to admit it was nice to feel a cool temperature without freezing. He didn't have to pile on layers or power through the snow like he did in New York. He could get used to it. Orlando was very different from the big city, but maybe it could be home. He promised himself that he was going to give it a fair shot. Plus, he wanted to be far away from Holly, no matter how uncomfortable that would be.

When he arrived at the taco place, the line was so long he almost had to stand outside. He scanned the menu above the register and settled on the fish tacos, his favorite. There was a little place near his apartment in New York that he used to go to. That was one of the things he would miss the most—that and…

"Next!" the cashier said. He snapped out of his trance, placed his order, and was lucky enough to find a seat near the window. It was the only one left because a couple was getting up just as he finished ordering.

He sat down and took off his jacket. He could relax now after getting the apartment sorted. The easy going pace of Orlando was also refreshing. In New York, the restaurants were a different kind of busy. People rushed to get from one place to the next. Here, the restaurant itself was busy from the amount of people, but the people themselves were at leisure.

The door opened, and a gust of wind swirled in. He shivered, then blinked a few times when *she* walked in. It was the woman he had bumped into earlier. His first inclination was to think, what are the odds of that? Then he remembered he wasn't that far from the apartment. He was bound to run into her again.

Crap. He had almost put the incident behind him, but there she was making him feel bad all over again. Her eyes met his then.

She had bewitching umber eyes. He shook the thought away and then raised his hand to wave. She narrowed her eyes and gave a reluctant wave back. He knew nothing about her, but he could gather that she was guarded.

She had gone back to searching the menu above, so Charlie pulled out his phone to check through his email again. He had a couple weeks off to get situated, but he didn't want to fall too far behind. When he looked up, it was just in time to see the woman hop out of line with her table number in hand. She searched the room for an empty table, but there weren't any. Again he caught her eye. Before he could even think about it, he motioned to the empty chair at his table and smiled. What was he doing? No doubt she would think he was a creep. First, he practically knocked her over this morning, and now he expected her to basically join him for dinner?

She shook her head, then mouthed,

"It's okay."

"Come on," he said from across the room, "I don't bite." The room wasn't that big, so many of the diners turned to observe. She gave a half-smile and made her way over.

"Do you always embarrass women like that, or do you usually have luck with that being part of your charm?" she asked, setting her number down on the table.

A laugh escaped his lips. She was bold, and he liked it.

"Glad I can entertain you," she said, removing her jacket and sitting down in the seat across from him.

He couldn't take the smile off his face. "I'm sorry. I wasn't trying to embarrass you. I was just trying to help," he said.

She narrowed her eyes for the second time that evening.

"I'm Charlie Palmer," he said, extending his arm across the table and hoping he could dissolve some of her suspicion.

She waited another few seconds before reaching for his hand. "Viola Evans."

A flicker of electric energy sparked as

he held her hand, then charged through his entire body. He didn't want to let go. She held on a second longer and then pulled her hand back. He tried not to cringe as he thought about how weird he was being.

"Viola is a nice name," he said.

She shrugged and glanced back at the register.

"Look, I'm really sorry about this morning. I should have been watching where I was going," he said. He loosened his jaw and tried to relax his face to show her he meant what he said.

She kept her expression stony for a beat longer, then softened. "Don't worry about it," she said.

He let out a deep breath. "So, what did you order?" he asked.

"The tofu tacos. You?" she said. She kept her shoulders square and sat up straight. He wondered if she ever relaxed.

"I got the chicken," he said, clearing his throat. "Are you a vegetarian?" he asked.

"I am," she said. She shifted in her chair. "So, where are you moving from? I've never seen you around the building."

"New York. Got a transfer in my

company," he said.

"And what do you do?"

"I'm an actuary," he said, smiling. "Just another numbers geek."

She laughed just as the server brought her tacos to the table.

So she laughs, he thought. Her laugh echoed in his ears, and his heart contracted. He ignored it.

"What do you do?" he asked.

"I work at a center for children without families, and I'm a freelance illustrator," she said, biting into one of her tacos. "I'm really hungry," she said, between chews.

"Same," he said, taking a bite of his. "So is that where you're coming from? Work?" he asked.

"Yeah. It's a little later than usual. I sometimes stay longer, especially during the holidays. A little extra love can't hurt around this time, you know?" she said.

"I do. My parents were always traveling for work growing up. They still do, actually. Dad is a pilot, and Mom's his travel buddy. They were never big on the holidays, and I've learned to be grateful that takeout places are still open," he said.

"Wait, so you celebrate Christmas—"

"—Either alone or on the road. You get used to it after doing it for so long," Charlie said, shrugging.

"No singing Christmas carols, or decorating the tree, or… Christmas donuts?" Viola asked.

"Christmas what?"

"You can't be serious. You've never had a Christmas donut? You know, red or green frosting, cute holiday sprinkles?"

"I think we had a tree once," Charlie said, taking a sip of water. "And I don't really do donuts. I'm not big on sweets."

"You're not living," Viola said, a smirk playing at her lips.

"I take it you love Christmas?" he asked. There was definitely a softer side to Viola.

"I love Christmas, even wrote letters to Santa today with the kids at work. It made me feel like a kid again. When did we all stop believing in magic?" she said, swallowing another bite of her taco.

"Oh yeah? So what did you ask Santa for?"

She paused. "If I tell you, I'll have to

kill you."

He almost spit out the bite of taco he had in his mouth. "That's a bit extreme," he said between laughs.

She cracked a smile. "Just kidding. If I tell you it won't come true," she said.

"I see. Well, Viola Evans, I hope you get your Christmas wish," he said. He stared into her eyes, and she didn't look away. He felt a pull towards her, and didn't know what to make of it. It was confusing, especially since sometimes feelings for Holly lingered.

Viola snapped out of it first. She finished the last bite of her taco and said, "Well, I gotta get going. Thanks for letting me hang out at your table."

"Oh, no problem," he said as he watched her put her jacket back on.

"I'm sure I'll see you around. We live in the same building after all," she said.

"Yeah, for sure."

"Welcome to Orlando." And with that, she picked up her tray and was out the door.

He replayed the conversation in his head. He had a feeling there was more to Viola Evans than what met the eye. He stood up to clear his table and noticed a red envelope on the seat where Viola sat. Was it hers, or was it a previous patron's, and neither one of them noticed? He picked it up and flipped it over. The word Santa was written on the back. Viola had mentioned writing a letter to Santa. The flap wasn't sealed. Deep down, he knew he shouldn't read it, but he was curious. He lifted the flap, pulled the letter out, and unfolded it.

Dear Santa,

This Christmas, I'm writing to you with a bit of a broken heart. I thought I'd be spending this holiday season with the love of my life, but that isn't the case. It's been ten months since my breakup with Mark, and honestly, I should be over it. Maybe I'm just holding on because it's easy.

I have a two-part wish. The first is to finally have a healed heart. I don't know, maybe the holiday spirit will rub off on me? I've always loved Christmas, and it might be the perfect time to remind me about all the truly important things. The second part of my wish is to maybe meet someone new. I know this one is trickier—and I'm not expecting to fall in love—but it would be great not to spend the holidays alone. Maybe someone who likes the same things as me: Christmas donuts, and dancing to Christmas music, and likes to drive around neighborhoods looking at lights. I know that's asking a lot, but my heart is on the page here, and I figured I'd ask. Thanks for considering me, Santa.

Love,
Your long-time fan,
Viola

Charlie folded the letter back up and tucked it into the envelope. So he was right. There was more to Viola Evans. If he doubted the connection he felt to her before, he didn't now. She was bruised just like he was. That would also explain the bit of edginess when he bumped into her earlier.

He wanted to make it better for her, somehow it didn't matter that he had just met her. Then again, what was he supposed to say? *Hey, Viola, I found your letter to Santa, and I think I can be that guy at least for the holiday season?* She'd really think he was a creep then. He was beginning to think the same thing. Should he give the letter back to her or leave it here? It wasn't like he had any contact information for her. They lived in the same apartment building, but it could be weeks before he bumped into her again.

He sighed and placed the letter in his coat pocket. The string of thoughts that had just weaved through his brain couldn't be normal. Still, he was very much intrigued by Viola Evans.

Viola

It was already 11:45 a.m., and Viola had to be downstairs at noon to help Mrs. Walker in the leasing office. After living here for three years, she had worn Mrs. Walker down, and the two had developed a friendship. Mrs. Walker had mentioned needing help to complete the decorating in the leasing office. Her exact words were that she "was no spring chicken." Viola jumped at the chance to distract her mind. Anything was better than moping around her apartment and staring at that sapphire ring. She hadn't even wanted a sapphire ring to begin with—Mark just assumed.

Viola had spent the last few days looking for the letter she wrote to Santa at The Center last week. She didn't think to look for it when she got home from dinner that day, but it came across her mind, and when she reached for it in her coat pocket, it was gone. She prayed it slipped out somewhere on the street and not at the restaurant. She would be mortified if Charlie got a hold of it. If he did find it, she hoped he wouldn't read it. And she couldn't very well ask him if he found it. It would be too embarrassing to admit she was serious about this letter. And then what if he *had* read it? She shook the thought away. It was probably lost on the street and whisked off somewhere. Who knows, it might even be in the trash by now.

After finishing breakfast, she hurried to the elevator. It wasn't long before it dinged to signal she was now on the first floor. The heavy doors whooshed open, and she stepped out. It was nice and quiet today since it was a Saturday. Everyone was probably out Christmas shopping or spending time with loved ones.

She opened the door to the front office, and it jingled like sleigh bells. Viola glanced around.

"You like?" Mrs. Walker said from behind her desk. She had on shiny gold reindeer antlers and a holiday sweater with tiny colorful gift bows.

"Wow, you're really getting into the spirit of things, aren't you?" Viola asked. She inhaled deeply and took in the pine scent that filled the space.

"It's never too early. The holiday season will be over before you know it. How are you, dear?" she asked.

"Same old," Viola said, tying her long curly hair up.

"Don't tell me it's that jerk, Mark, again. He was never good enough for you, and I only met him one time," Mrs. Walker said.

"I know, I know. Logically, I get that," Viola said, her lips turning down into a frown.

"But the heart wants what the heart wants, right?" she asked.

"Yeah. Except, I don't think my heart or my brain knows what it wants," Viola said.

"Sure they do. You're just not listening. You're too busy fighting," Mrs. Walker said.

She had a point there. No matter what she did, she couldn't quiet her mind. Her brain could have been a busy city street complete with sirens, car horns, and her endless thoughts cluttering the sidewalks.

"I can see your wheels turning. Let's try to live in the now as you young kids would say," Mrs. Walker said, snickering.

Viola joined her in the laughing fit, but it was interrupted by the sleigh bells at the door. They both turned their heads. Charlie stood in the doorway with a huge smile on his face, a smile that made Viola's heart abandon steady beats. Viola wondered if it was because he knew about the letter. What if he found the letter and was mocking her right now? She was being ridiculous.

"Sorry to interrupt, but the pipe under the kitchen sink is leaking, and I wanted to see if I could talk to anyone about it?" he said, focusing his attention on Mrs. Walker.

Mrs. Walker rolled her eyes. She grabbed a form from the stackable organizational trays on her desk and held it out. "Fill out this work order," she said.

"More paperwork?" Charlie asked, wrinkling his forehead.

"Could you be lazier?" she said, rolling her eyes again. "Fill it out if you want it fixed. We have to keep records, buddy."

He sighed.

Violet giggled. He was kind of cute when he was frustrated. He smiled when he noticed her staring, and she held her breath on instinct. Why did those golden-brown eyes have to be such magnets?

"I guess you're getting a kick out of this," he said, making his way over to the table. "What are you two doing in here anyway?" He surveyed the room.

"Decorating if you must know, Mr. nosy pants," Mrs. Walker said.

"Ohhhh. Need any help?" he asked.

Now both women looked at each other and then narrowed their eyes at him.

"You want to help?" they both said in unison.

"Sure, looks like a lot of fun," he said, placing the paper on the desk and rolling up the sleeves of his pinstriped dress shirt.

Viola again held her breath as she noticed his toned arms. Her mind drifted to the letter again. If he read it, he wasn't acting like it. She needed to let it go. At some point, she needed to accept that not everyone needed a background check.

Mrs. Walker picked up a thick piece of garland and pushed it against his chest. "Here, you can start by climbing on the ladder and hanging this."

Charlie flashed a smile at her and then Viola. Viola tried harder to ignore the rise of electricity in her body. What was that? Nope. She wasn't going there. She couldn't allow herself to even have the slightest bit of attraction to some random guy from New York. She knew nothing about him beyond their dinner conversation from last week. And what if he wanted to go back to New York?

"Earth to Viola," Mrs. Walker said, breaking into her thoughts. She stood in front of Viola with a slight smirk on her face.

"Oh, what did you say?" Viola asked, blinking her eyes.

"Are you going to help me make the wreath for the office door or not?" she asked.

"Right. Yes, of course," Viola said, taking the large wreath from Mrs. Walker.

Mrs. Walker set a plastic box down on the coffee table in the waiting area.

"Here, these are the little ornaments and decorations you can use to spruce it up," she said.

"Okay, great," Viola said, opening the lid and peering inside. She took out a tiny present box and stuck it into the wreath.

Mrs. Walker nodded her head. "While you do that, I'm going to arrange the poinsettias in the pots so we can place them around the room. I just need to grab them from my car. You two think you can handle this without your supervisor for a few minutes?" She placed her hands on her hips and winked.

"Aye, Aye, Captain," Viola said.

Charlie saluted.

There was a bit of an awkward silence once Mrs. Walker left, but Viola decided to be direct.

"So, Charlie, what made you decide to take the job here in Orlando? That must have been a tough decision," she said, continuing to add decorations to the wreath.

"Well, it was mostly work," he said, climbing the ladder to hang the garland near the ceiling.

"Key word there being mostly," Viola

said.

He drew in a deep breath. "Right. If I'm being totally honest, I wanted to get away from my ex. Needed a fresh start," he said.

Viola's chest tightened. That word ex made her uncomfortable these days. She couldn't hear it without tensing.

Charlie continued, "Her name was Holly. She wanted to see other people. I'm not really sure what happened with us, other than she said it just wasn't working for her. *No chemistry,* I think were her exact words." He kept his attention on his task.

"No chemistry? But didn't she feel chemistry in the beginning to go out with you?"

"One would think so, wouldn't they?" he said.

"I'm sorry," Viola said, keeping her eyes focused on the wreath she was decorating. "This should make you feel better. Try thinking you were going to spend the rest of your life with the love of your life, and he proposes only to call it off shortly after."

"Cold feet?"

"That's what I thought. Maybe he got really nervous when he realized we'd be committing to spending an eternity together. That was ten months ago. If he had cold feet, they must be frozen by now," Viola said. She giggled. It was the first time she laughed about her story since the breakup.

"A beautiful woman like you? It was definitely his loss," Charlie said, meeting her eyes.

At first, Viola couldn't look away. Something swirled through her, something that scared her. She broke the trance. "Your ex suffered a loss, too," she said, digging through the box so she wouldn't have to look at him.

Charlie smiled and continued working on the garland. He cleared his throat. "You, uh, you have dinner plans this evening?" he asked.

Viola's hands seized movement. For a second, she couldn't move. "I don't," she said, keeping her voice as even as she could.

"Would you want to join me for dinner? You'd have to choose the restaurant. I know nothing about Orlando," he said, a nervous laugh escaping his lips. He kept his eyes on the garland.

Viola's whole body tensed. She was afraid to answer. She had so much freelance work to do, including figuring out the extra decorations for the center. She should say no.

Charlie glanced at her and fiddled with the garland some more.

"I'd like that," she said. She let the words catapult out before she could change her mind.

Charlie smiled. "And maybe you can show me some of the lights in the neighborhood after?" he said.

Viola smiled. "After dinner? Might be getting a little late after we eat," she said, raising an eyebrow.

"Live a little," Charlie said.

She couldn't help but smile. "Okay."

"Meet in the lobby at seven?" he asked.

"Sure," she said.

"It's a date."

Was it?

Charlie

Charlie got off the elevator exactly twenty minutes earlier than the scheduled time. What was he thinking? A woman like Viola was out of his league. She was beautiful, smart, and kind. He couldn't even remember the last time he volunteered. And what if he messed this up like he messed up his last relationship? It's just dinner, not a relationship, he told himself. *Calm down, Charlie.* There wasn't anything to mess up since Viola was just a woman he was having dinner with. That's all.

He was staring out the large window when the elevator dinged behind him. He took in Viola's reflection in the glass as she stepped out of the double doors, and his heart skipped. It was only a paper thin image of her, and still, his heart had betrayed his mind. He turned around, and there was Viola, who shimmered under the light from the lobby's chandelier.

He learned not to stare as a child, but he was starting to notice there seemed to always be something magnetic about Viola Evans. It would be easy for him to say it was her appearance, that she didn't look like other women. That she was more beautiful than them even. But that would be too easy. It was more than that. What was beautiful about Viola was her energy and warmth. He felt it every time she walked in the room.

"You look…amazing," he said.

She smiled, and a subtle rose color surfaced at the height of her brown cheeks. "Thank you," she said. She glanced at him for only a second and then looked away.

Was he laying it on too thick? "Ready to go?" he asked.

"Yeah," she said.

He held the door to the apartment building open for her, and the two of them made their way to the car.

The ride over was fairly quiet as the GPS did most of the talking. He had insisted on putting it on, though Viola said she could direct him. He figured it would be good background noise since he was so nervous for some reason. Viola talked about the lights on some of the houses, and he thought it was adorable how much she loved Christmas.

When they arrived at the restaurant, the parking lot was full. "Wow, I didn't expect it to be this busy on a weeknight," he said, putting his blinker on as they stumbled on someone backing out of a spot.

"Lazy Moon is always busy. It doesn't matter what night of the week it is. It's a local staple," Viola said, unbuckling her seatbelt.

"I love eating at local namesakes," he said.

Inside was just as busy as the parking lot, but much brighter. He took in the menu and realized it was a pizza joint. "I wasn't expecting pizza," he whispered to Viola. He was used to most of the women he dated picking some of the most expensive restaurants in New York City. Holly would never suggest date night at a pizza restaurant. Then again, this wasn't a date.

"You asked for my favorite restaurant,

did you not?" Viola said, furrowing her brows.

"I did," he smiled. She was refreshing, and something about her made him feel not so dead. Was it possible to feel that after just a couple conversations?

They placed their order and found two empty seats at one of Lazy Moon's giant community tables.

"This place is pretty cool," Charlie said. He took off his jacket and sipped from his cup of coke. He observed that all the employees wore Santa hats. He was starting to think Orlando took Christmas pretty seriously.

"Told ya," Viola said, her lips spreading into a smirk.

The waitress came over and set down two colossal slices of pizza. "I don't think I've ever seen a slice of pizza this big," Charlie said. He stared at the pizza in awe as the scent of pepperoni tempted his nostrils.

"Wait until you take a bite," Viola said.

"It's impossible to eat this with your hands. Like, I'm forced to use a knife and fork," he said.

"Exactly," Viola said. She picked up the circular tray that her veggie slice was on. "Look at all this delicious goodness."

Charlie dug in and took a bite. "Mmm. Oh my God, that's amazing. You were right again. This could give so many pizza joints in New York a run for their money," he said.

"I hate to sound like a broken record, but I told you," Viola said, her mouth full of extra cheese and veggies.

"Now I get why this is your favorite place to eat," he said. Now that I know where it is, I have a feeling I'm going to be spending a lot more time in the gym," he said.

"You'll be a local in no time," Viola said, her voice playful.

He was having such a good time with her. And they weren't even doing much. It was easy going: Viola, the restaurant, the pizza. All they seemed to be doing was enjoying a meal, and it was the most relaxed and free he'd been in years. It might have been odd for him to be thinking about his past, but all of this made him wonder what he'd been doing. It was like his life before moving here had somehow been discredited. It took this very moment, this pizza place—Viola—for him to notice everything before now somehow felt... insufficient.

"Where did you go?" Viola asked, bringing him back to the present.

He swallowed a bite of pizza and hesitated before saying, "I'm sorry, I didn't mean to check out for a moment."

"Oh, it's okay. I didn't take it personally. But are you okay?" she asked.

"Yeah. It's just that this move has been an unexpected eye-opener," he said.

She raised an eyebrow. "How so?"

"Well, I didn't expect to be reflecting on my life in a pizza joint," he said, an uncomfortable laugh escaping. "But everything about this night has been pretty easy. It's been uncomplicated, which is the opposite of my life. I'm having a good time," he said, looking into her eyes.

There. It was out, and a part of what was inside of him hung in the air between them. Given her own past, it might have been too much for her. But he had to say *something*.

"I'm having a really great time, too," she said, their eyes melding together. "I haven't been able to relax like this since…" she looked down at what was left of her pizza. "Since, you know."

He definitely knew. "You don't have to say it. I know exactly what you mean."

The silence they shared for the next few seconds felt comfortable, like they'd somehow just realized they knew each other for a lifetime.

"Should we walk around the neighborhood? I'd love to see some lights," Charlie said, draining his coke.

"Sure—but only for a little. I have to be at the center early," Viola said.

"Got it," Charlie said. He stood up and took her hand to help her up. It was the second time their hands had touched, and he wasn't expecting yet another spark. That wasn't supposed to happen a second time.

"So why Christmas?" Charlie asked once they were outside. The cool air swirled around them and whipped through Viola's curls. It made her even more stunning.

"Before I lost my parents in the accident, Christmas was our favorite family holiday. We had so many family traditions," she said, gazing into the distance as they walked. "My mom loved donuts. She and my dad met in a donut shop in college, actually. They both wanted the last Jelly donut." She laughed.

"Who got the donut?" Charlie asked, his tone playful.

"They split it," Viola said, glancing at him.

"So is that why you asked if I'd ever had a Christmas donut?"

"Yeah. Christmas donuts were an Evans family tradition. Mom made a lot of them throughout the season, and we'd decorate them together. Christmas, the donuts—it all makes me feel a little closer to them even though they aren't here," she said.

"Kind of makes me want to have a real Christmas," Charlie said, surprising himself.

"Everyone should have a real Christmas. You might be off to a good start," Viola said, stopping in front of a house with what seemed like a million lights. Every inch of house and lawn and tree was lit up in white lights.

The house itself was impressive, but Charlie couldn't peel his eyes off of Viola, who marveled at the sight before them.

"This has to be the most enchanting thing I've ever seen," Viola said.

"It sure is," Charlie said, but he wasn't talking about the house.

When they finally arrived back to the apartment building, Charlie said, "Can I walk you to your door? Just to make sure you get in safely?"

A slight smile played at Viola's lips. "You do realize I walk myself to my door on a regular basis, right?"

"Still, you're out late with me. It would put my mind at ease," he said, sticking his hands in his pockets. Why was his heart beating so fast? It was just a question.

"Okay," Viola said.

They were quiet on the elevator ride up to Viola's apartment on the seventh floor. Once they were in front of her door, Viola said, "Well, thanks for walking me up. I know I gave you a hard time downstairs, but it was really sweet of you," she said.

"My pleasure. Thank you for a nice

night," Charlie said.

"You wouldn't want to go help me at The Center next week, would you? It's the one job where you're allowed to bring people to work, and we're doing another holiday activity with the kids," she said. She kept her eyes on him.

"I'd love to," he said.

Viola's face brightened. "Great! We can meet downstairs and maybe ride over to the center together?" she asked.

"Sounds like a plan," Charlie said.

She looked beautiful in the hallway light. It wasn't even the best lighting, but her presence turned everything bright. He really wanted to kiss her and he once again felt her magnetism. Somehow, they had drifted toward each other and were now standing pretty close. He leaned a little closer, and so did Viola, but his phone buzzed in his pocket. At first, neither of them moved. Their eyes stayed locked for a few beats longer until Charlie finally decided the moment was lost.

The two of them laughed. "I guess that's my cue. I'll see you later," he said.

"Yeah, see ya," Viola said. She went

inside and closed the door.

Charlie let out a deep breath.

"Darn phone," he said, taking it out of his pocket to see who had interrupted. He clicked the side button to light up the screen, and there was a text message. His heart stopped as he read the name: Holly.

Letter to Santa

Viola

A week later, Viola tried to calm the rise in her stomach. Why was she so nervous? She was going to work just like any other day. Except, it wasn't any other day. Charlie was going with her today.

She replayed their dinner in her mind a thousand times. She thought she would never feel that again—the rise and fall of each of her heartbeats. It was astounding how heartbeats were simply routines of the body—they kept a person alive after all. But then someone could enter your life, and suddenly you felt every single beat. Suddenly there was a tempo, those beats turning into energy and igniting every one of your cells.

She shook her head—she was getting ahead of herself. Was she imagining it? And that night he had leaned in closer, and she had too. Had they almost—no. It was in her head. It had to be.

As she walked to the lobby, she glanced inside the leasing office to see Mrs. Walker settling down at her desk with her morning cup of coffee. She checked the time. She still had a few moments before Charlie would be down to meet her. She pushed the door open, and the sleigh bells jingled.

"Morning," she said to Mrs. Walker, shutting the door behind her.

"Morning! Aren't we in a chipper mood," Mrs. Walker said. She smirked and sipped from her *Kiss Me I'm an Elf* mug.

"Chipper? What? I'm my normal self," Viola said.

"Viola, cut the crap. You know I'm not one for sugar coating things. You're extra happy today. It's all over your face. You've been moping around here for the past ten months. Today you're different. Look," she said, pointing to Viola's shoulders, "your shoulders aren't slumped like they normally are. And you've got a big goofy smile on your face. You forget that I've been on this planet a bit longer than you, dear." She sat back in her chair, folded her hands, and placed them on her chest.

"I don't know what you're talking about," Viola said, trying to hide her smile.

"Ha! I'm not going to ask you again, Viola Evans. I have a feeling this has something to do with Charlie."

"What? No way," Viola said, waving a hand in the air.

"No? So you're saying that your date last week didn't go well?" Mrs. Walker asked, raising an eyebrow.

"It wasn't a date. And how did you—"

"How did I know you had a date? Just remember, I'm the Queen Bee of this office. I know everything," she said.

Viola let out a deep laugh this time. "Okay, Queen Bee," she said, between laughs. She laughed so hard she could barely breathe.

"Quit stalling, and tell me about the date," Mrs. Walker said. Her tone was a bit more serious this time.

"First, it wasn't a date. But we did have a good time," Viola said, her voice dreamlike.

"I knew it. You've got the hots for this guy," Mrs. Walker said.

Viola gasped. "I do not!" she said.

"Sure," Mrs. Walker said with a sly smile.

"I, I can't," Viola said. "I've got a full life, and I have no time to date. I'm already behind on my freelance work. Where would I find time in my schedule for a boyfriend?" Viola said.

"Those are excuses, Viola. You know very well, you're just afraid to say what you feel out loud," Mrs. Walker said. She opened the candy jar she kept on her desk and popped a peppermint into her mouth.

"Isn't it a bit early for candy?" Viola asked.

"Deflecting," Mrs. Walker said as she chewed.

"Fine. Maybe I do feel something. But it doesn't have to mean anything. I had a good time. Doesn't mean we're getting married," she said.

"But you could."

"You're insufferable!"

"Viola, don't blow this. It's time you let go of what's his name. He didn't deserve you. Don't mess up a chance at something good. I want you to be happy," Mrs. Walker said. She kept her gaze intense so Viola would know she was serious.

"What if he doesn't feel the same way? And what if I'm meant to be alone? When Mark called off our engagement, I kept thinking that maybe I wasn't supposed to be attached. Maybe I'm supposed to serve the world and be a loner," she said, taking a seat on one of the waiting room chairs.

"That's bull, and you know it. You're worthy of being loved. If you think otherwise, you've created that narrative for yourself. Don't assume you'll fail before you even try. You owe it to yourself to see where this could go. He seems like a good guy," Mrs. Walker said.

"You think he's a good guy? You gave him such a hard time," Viola said, wrinkling her brows.

"I give everyone a hard time. It's who I am." Mrs. Walker chuckled and took a giant gulp of her coffee. "Besides, it's all in the reaction. He never once told me off, and let's be honest, he could have."

"I just don't want to get my hopes up," Viola said.

"Get your hopes up, honey. Not getting

your hopes up is something people say because they want to brace themselves for disappointment. I have a good feeling about this. Just try not to put too much pressure on it and see where it takes you."

"Maybe you're right."

Sleigh bells jingled and Charlie walked in.

"Good morning, ladies," he said, flashing a smile.

He had a slight dimple in his right cheek, and Viola wondered why she hadn't noticed it before. It was subtle, something you might have to look close to notice. She tried to ignore the way the beats of her heart bolted in real time.

"Morning," Mrs. Walker said. "You two better get out of here or you'll be late. Be young and free," she said. She winked at Viola.

"You all set?" Charlie said, switching his attention to Viola.

"Yeah," she said, standing up and positioning her purse on her shoulder.

"See you later," Mrs. Walker said, drawing out the last word and taking the pitch up an octave higher than necessary.

Viola glared at her. "Bye," she said through gritted teeth.

Christmas music blared through the speakers of Charlie's car as they drove to the center.

"I didn't take you for the Christmas music kind of guy," Viola said, tapping her fingers to *Sleigh Ride*.

"I'm usually not," he said, glancing at her from the corner of his eye.

"So what's up with the change?" she asked.

"I don't know. Maybe the fresh start. This city that feels like home somehow. *You*," he said.

It was the way he said you, and how close it was to the word home. His words were a match that set everything inside of her ablaze.

"Me?" she asked. She needed to make sure she heard him right.

"Yeah. *You*," he said again. Now it was clear, which made her want to tell him to pull over so she could wrap her arms around him. Everything in her tingled.

"I—" She struggled to find something to say. She wanted to say the right thing, but what?

"You don't have to say anything, you know," Charlie said. His expression was gentle.

She smiled and relaxed. Maybe Mrs. Walker was right. This was a chance at something new, something good even. Maybe she needed to choose the path to Charlie Palmer.

Charlie

Charlie was so impressed with the kids at the center. They were a smart, sharp, and creative bunch. He knew exactly why Viola liked working here. They were in the middle of a pretty intense book club discussion on *The Polar Express* when he looked up and caught Viola's eye. She led the discussion while everyone sat in a circle. She was mesmerizing. No matter how much he tried to resist her magic, he couldn't. Maybe it was time to stop ignoring it. The night he walked her to her door, he had wanted to kiss her so badly. His desire had been different, more charged. He hadn't even come close to feeling like that before. Now that he was getting to know Viola, somehow the time with Holly felt hollow.

A young girl with dark hair and freckles tapped him on the arm. "Hey, Mister," she said.

"Hello," Charlie said, smiling.

"The lit discussion is over," she said, pointing to the crowd of kids dispersing.

"I guess I was wrapped up in my own thoughts," Charlie said. He wondered if he should have admitted that. He was supposed to be checked in while he was here, not checked out.

"That's pretty clear," she said, a bit more edge in her voice.

Charlie laughed. "What's your name anyway?" he asked.

"Lang," she said.

"It's nice to meet you, Lang," Charlie said.

"Hey, you two," Viola said, approaching them both.

"I was just introducing myself to Lang here," Charlie said.

"Oh, that's great! Lang is awesome," Viola said.

"Are you Viola's boyfriend?" Lang asked.

There was an awkward pause, but then both Charlie and Viola laughed this time.

They stumbled over words before Viola

finally said, "Charlie and I are new friends. He moved here from New York and lives in the same apartment building as I do."

"Is that how you guys met?" Lang asked, her deep brown eyes twinkling.

"Yeah, except you forgot the part about me almost knocking you over," he said, his smile softening.

"Well, I think you made up for it," Viola said, meeting his gaze and then looking away.

"You two should get married," Lang said. She continued staring at the pair like they were a Christmas movie couple.

"You might be getting a bit ahead of yourself, Lang," Viola said. She shifted her attention to Charlie. "She's a hopeless romantic."

"Nothing wrong with that," Charlie said. He held Viola's gaze, daring her to look away. She didn't.

"See?" Lang said, her smile wide.

"Alright, why don't you go join the others," Viola said.

Lang kept her smile, then disappeared down the hall.

"Cute kid," Charlie said.

"Too cute," Viola said, blushing. She made her way to the front of the center. "You ready to head out?" she asked.

"Sure. This was really fun. I'm glad I came."

"I'm glad you came too," Viola said, touching his arm.

It sent a shiver through him, and he brushed it off, blamed it on the chilly gust of air that came through when he opened the front door. "I was going to grab my first Christmas donut and take a walk around downtown—maybe even look at some more Christmas lights. I don't suppose you might be interested in joining me?" he asked.

Viola's eyes widened. "So you're into Christmas donuts now, huh?"

"This really beautiful local has inspired me to give it a try," Charlie said, tilting his head to one side.

Viola thought for a second. Charlie observed as her thoughts flashed in her eyes. She could easily brush him off. She could do anything else in the world like finish her Christmas shopping, or wrap Christmas gifts, or make cookies for The Center's upcoming Christmas party, or catch up on work. There were a million other things she might want to do more than hang out with him, and this whole moment could blow up in his face.

"I do have a little bit of time before I have to get back home," Viola said, and he couldn't help but notice the way her smile glowed.

"Great," Charlie said, trying to keep his voice steady.

It wasn't that late in the day, and they were able to find parking downtown with no trouble, which was usually tricky. They walked to one of the little bakeries, ordered their donuts, and were back out on the street in a matter of minutes.

"I love when it's not too busy downtown," Viola said, taking a bite of her red frosted donut. "Mmm," she said, closing her eyes for a second as she chewed.

Charlie tasted his chocolate frosted donut with red and green sprinkles. "Oh, that's good," he said, licking the frosting from his lips. "This is so different from New York. There's no such thing as the city being quiet. There are clearly people moving around here, but the calm is unlike anything I'm used to," he said.

"I don't know how you did it. That kind of city life is not my cup of tea," Viola said.

"Florida girl to the end, huh," Charlie said.

"Yup," Viola said. "Palm trees and flip flops, and Mickey Mouse." She giggled.

"Those aren't bad things," Charlie said.

"Do you miss New York?" Viola asked as a Lynx bus whooshed past them.

"I did at first, but the more I spend time here, the more I like it. And the company has been particularly exceptional," he said. He kept his eyes forward.

She smiled. "The company is something, isn't it?" she said.

Charlie felt that jump inside of him again. What was Viola doing to him? "You ever been to New York?" he asked.

"Once, when I was really young. I don't remember much, though," she said.

"Maybe one day I'll get to show you my favorite spots. It's only fair," he said.

"Yeah?"

"Yeah," Charlie said. He held his breath as he thought about what he was proposing.

He had implied a possible future between them without actually meaning to do that. What if she thought he was being too forward? He could definitely see himself taking this, whatever it was, a little further, but he also didn't want to scare her—or himself. His heart was charging ahead at full speed, but his brain was having trouble keeping up.

"I'd love to see the city with you," Viola said.

Still, neither of them looked at each other, but that confirmation made him feel a trillion times better. She at least didn't think he was some psycho for suggesting it. That's all that mattered.

"Oooh, what's that?" Viola asked, pointing ahead.

"I don't know. You're the townie," he said.

She rolled her eyes. "It looks like a few local musicians just wanted to get together to play music," she said, her eyes sparkling. "They do that sometimes."

"How nice," Charlie said.

As they got closer, the song became clearer. It was *Have Yourself a Merry Little*

Christmas. There was a singer with a raspy voice and two others on the trumpet and the keyboard.

"I love this song," Viola said.

Charlie paused for a second to muster up enough courage, and then asked, "Would you like to dance?" He held his hand out. The musicians nodded to them. There was no way Viola could refuse now that they had been acknowledged, at least he hoped so.

She didn't say a word and stared at his palm. He almost lost the nerve and pulled his hand away, but then Viola took it. Charlie gently pulled her close and kept her hand in his. His heart raced as he held her, and they slow danced to the mild rhythm of the song. Did she feel it? The air was chilly, but he felt none of it. He was on fire, and there was no mistaking what was happening. He was falling for Viola and he could try to talk himself out of it, but it would be no use.

Viola rested her head on his chest and closed her eyes. Again his heart stampeded. Now he wondered if she could hear it. Her ear was so close to it she must have.

He didn't want to leave this moment. He wanted to tuck it into his pocket and carry it with him all the time.

The song ended, and the quiet enveloped them. Viola took her time opening her eyes, which made him believe she enjoyed the dance as much as he did. She smiled up at him, and all he could think about was how soft her red lips looked. He leaned down and brushed his lips against hers. When she didn't pull away, he pressed his lips to hers. She held the side of his face, and Charlie suddenly knew what magic was.

Viola pulled away first. "I—"

Was it too soon? "If you didn't want me to—"

"No, I wanted you to," Viola said.

He let out a breath. "Good," he said, tucking back the loose strands of hair around her face.

The three musicians clapped, finally taking them out of the trance.

Charlie thought as they walked back to the car. Viola had kissed him back. That wasn't always an indication that a woman felt the same. Holly was a case in point. He might not have been one hundred percent sure of Viola's feelings, but one thing was certain, he was not the same Charlie he was when they arrived downtown—or the same Charlie that arrived in Orlando a couple weeks ago.

They were both quiet on the drive home. They had to sit with the transformation that just took place. As they got closer to the door of the apartment building, Charlie decided he had to speak up. He had to tell Viola how he felt right this second. It was a risk, but he had never felt like this ever. It had to be real, right? He reached for her hand and laced his fingers with hers.

"Viola, I have to tell you something—"

"Charlie?" a voice said up ahead. He squinted, and the blood drained from his face as he made out the figure waiting at the door to the building.

"Holly?" he whispered, his hands suddenly cold.

Viola

Viola leaned over to Charlie and whispered, "Who's that?" She was afraid of the answer, but she asked anyway.

Charlie let out a deep breath. "That would be my ex," he said.

He looked at Viola, but she couldn't meet his eye. She didn't want to know what kind of emotion was there. Was there a longing for Holly now that she was here resurrecting memories?

"Holly, what are you doing here?" Charlie asked once they made it to the front door where Holly stood.

Charlie's ex was exactly as Viola had expected: dark cascading waves of hair draped over her shoulders, long legs that only looked more elegant in the sleek high heels she wore. Her brown skin didn't have a single blemish. She was perfect.

Holly glanced at Viola and then continued. "Didn't you get any of my text messages?" she asked.

"Sort of," he said, looking into the distance.

"In my last one I told you I was going to come if you didn't respond," she said.

Viola let go of his hand. It felt like she was letting go of much more.

"How did you get my address?" Charlie asked.

"I have my ways, you know that," she said.

Charlie's shoulders slumped. He obviously knew what she was talking about. "Holly—"

"Can you not say anything now? Can we just talk," she said, glancing again at Viola, "privately."

Charlie sighed and then turned his whole body to Viola. "I have to take care of this, okay? Can I call you later?" he asked, his brows knitting together.

"Yeah, sure," Viola said. She tried to keep her tone light, hoping it covered up her disappointment.

Charlie half smiled. Great, now she

was officially part of the pity party. She walked through the large front doors and paused before walking to the elevators. When she turned around, she watched Holly and Charlie on the other side. Holly ran her hand up and down Charlie's arm, the outline of the door like a picture frame around the perfect snapshot of them.

Viola turned back around as her eyes burned. She needed to hurry and get on the elevator before she made a fool of herself in front of them. They would be in any second to ride the elevator up to Charlie's apartment. The last thing she needed was to be stuck on it with them. As soon as the elevator dinged, she hopped on and pushed the button to close the doors. She pressed her thumb to it and held not only the button, but her breath as she waited for the doors to shut. Meanwhile, her eyes blazed. Stupid elevator was all she could think as the doors finally shut after an eternity.

She let out a deep breath as the tears spilled out of her eyes. She couldn't believe how senseless she'd been. And this time, she had no one to blame but herself. Mark had blindsided her when he called off their engagement. This time, it was her own fault for catching feelings for Charlie when she knew how this could end. She let her guard down for two seconds, and now here she was.

Once she was in her apartment, she plopped down on the couch and cried until her eyes were sore. She was thankful that eyes didn't bruise—but hearts scarred, and here she was with another one.

She pictured Holly again. There was no way she could compete with that. Holly was a goddess. Viola had always viewed herself as more of a girl next door. And if that's who Charlie was attracted to initially, then Holly was obviously his type. Not Viola. Had she been imagining the attraction between them this whole time?

She sighed, embarrassed that she thought maybe there was something real between the two of them. He probably just got caught up in the moment. Now they were in the same apartment building, and she had to figure out how to avoid him. Maybe he'd move back to New York if he and Holly made up.

"It's all going to be okay," she repeated

to herself in the empty apartment. It had to be. Charlie had made her forget Mark so she could do this again. And they weren't even that involved. So they kissed. So what? She was an adult. New focus: forget Charlie Palmer.

Charlie

Charlie could have entered his thoughts in a NASCAR race. Right now, they spun out of control and were on the verge of a wreck.

He stood on the sidewalk in front of Holly, the cool wind circling them. "You still haven't answered my question, Holly. What are you doing here?"

Holly stuck out her bottom lip, and her eyes grew dewy. "I missed you. I had to come. You didn't even say goodbye," she said.

"Goodbye? You said goodbye to me, remember? Why would I tell you goodbye when you made it clear we were done?" he asked. He had been hurt by her actions at the time, but the truth was that she was selfish.

"Don't be like that. I was confused. I

didn't know what I wanted," she said.

"And you know that now?" he asked.

"I do. I'm sorry, babe." She took a step closer to him, narrowing the space between them. "I'm human. I made a mistake, but I'm not confused anymore."

Part of him wanted to believe her. It would be so easy to believe her and go back to the way things were. Except things weren't the way they were. His jaw tightened. Holly ran her hand over it, and instead of feeling a thrill like he used to, he felt nothing. He stiffened.

"Come on, don't be like that," she said. Now she closed the entire gap between them. She wrapped her arms around his neck and stood on her tiptoes to kiss him, but he placed both hands on her shoulders to stop her.

"Holly, I can't do this anymore," he said, his jaw still locked. He didn't want to be mean, but she hadn't considered his feelings when she broke up with him out of nowhere a few months ago.

She took a step back. "What?" she said, her sad expression turning sharp.

"I said I can't do this anymore. I know

I haven't been here long, but this move—this city—made something click. We were never right for each other. If we got back together, you'd be bored in a couple weeks. We'd end up broken up again," he said.

"I'm not going to be bored. Give me a little credit here," she said, running her fingers through her long hair.

"Let's say we get back together. Are you going to move here?" he said, leaning his head forward a bit.

"I, I guess I assumed you would come home to New York. I didn't expect you to be so… settled," she said, her gaze dropping to the ground.

"I like it here, and it's been good for me. Look, we had a great time together, but we aren't right for each other. And that's okay," Charlie said.

"But I flew all the way here for you," she said. She lifted her head now to meet his eyes.

"I don't want to hurt you, but I think you're afraid of being alone. Being with me is comfortable. I think we should leave things as they are," he said, his lips moving into a flat line.

"In other words, you want me to turn around and get on a plane back home—without you," she said.

Charlie nodded. After today's outing with Viola, he knew what he wanted. It was the clearest it's ever been.

"Okay," Holly said, breathing in and then out. "Do you think you could at least give me a ride to the airport?" she asked.

Charlie nodded. It was the least he could do. She hadn't cared at all about him when she called things off, but he did feel a little bad for her. The sooner he got rid of Holly, the sooner he could get back to Viola. He had to let her know how he felt.

Viola

Viola knew she shouldn't, but she watched Charlie and Holly from her seventh floor window just as they headed out. They looked perfect together. Better than she could ever look at his side. She drew in a breath as they continued walking towards the parking lot. Well, that was confirmation. They were definitely getting back together. They were probably headed to dinner.

"Everything happens for a reason," she said aloud. She switched her attention to her Christmas tree.

And he had helped her get over Mark. It was so different with Charlie. It was something she couldn't explain, but *knew*. Or at least thought she knew. Now that she had a taste of whatever it was, she at least understood why Mark wasn't the one. She wanted something real, and she was never going to settle for anything less. And maybe whatever it was she felt for Charlie was just the beginning. Maybe that was just supposed to teach her what *real* was like.

She needed to clear her head, get some dinner of her own. It would also be a good time to sneak out and a lower risk of running into Charlie and Holly since they were headed out.

She made her way onto the elevator and rode it down to the first floor. A few people hustled in through the main doors ahead. Just as she was passing the leasing office door, she caught a glimpse of Mrs. Walker, who saw her too, and motioned for her to come in.

She didn't feel like talking to anyone, but Mrs. Walker would insist by chasing her down anyway. She had done it before.

Sleigh bells rang through the air as she pushed the door open.

"Out with it," Mrs. Walker said as soon as the door slammed shut.

"With what?" Viola grumbled.

"The moment we made eye contact, I knew something was wrong. That's why I called you in here. Now spit it out," she said. She folded her arms across her chest.

"I'm honestly fine. Just one of those days, you know?"

"Bologna. Don't make me ask you again. My shift is almost over, and I don't have time for your Tom-foolery," Mrs. Walker said. She kept her gaze stony.

Viola let out a deep sigh and plopped down on one of the chairs. She wasn't quite ready to talk about this, but maybe it might make her feel better to vent.

"It's Charlie," Viola said at last.

"I knew it," Mrs. Walker said. "Go on." She unfolded her arms and leaned forward.

"I guess," Viola bit her bottom lip, "I guess I was starting to like him a little." That was not easy to admit out loud.

"And?"

"And I think he's going to get back with his ex," Viola said, sadness washing over her.

"Well what would make you think that?" Mrs. Walker said.

Viola glanced up at her antlers headband. "I can't take you seriously with antlers on your head," she said.

"Don't change the subject. I asked a

question," Mrs. Walker said.

"She showed up today. And he and I had a pretty stellar day. We even danced on the street downtown. When we got back home, she was outside," Viola said.

"I see," Mrs. Walker said, pressing her lips together.

"It's over. And I'm fine with it. I just need a little time to get over him," Viola said. "Always just a little more time," she mumbled.

"Viola, I want you to think about something. Could it be that you're misreading things?"

Viola opened her mouth to answer and then closed it. "I mean, that's possible…" She thought about everything that happened earlier, and it all still made her feel like a choice had been made.

"If it's possible, why are you getting so bent out of shape? Have you had a chance to talk to Charlie since then?" Mrs. Walker asked.

"No," Viola said, dragging the last part of the word out.

"Exactly. Don't you think you should wait until you talk to him before forming your own conclusions?" Mrs. Walker raised both of her eyebrows.

Viola studied the floor. She knew Mrs. Walker was right, even though she didn't want to admit it.

"You know I'm right," Mrs. Walker said.

"How do you do that?" Viola asked.

"Do what?"

"Read my mind?"

"Many, many years of experience, my dear. I've been at this post for a very long time," she said, winking.

Viola smiled. Mrs. Walker could always cheer her up, even if Viola wasn't always fully convinced that things were going to work out.

"Relax. Go do whatever it is you were going to do, but wait for Charlie. Don't write anything off until you talk to him. If he makes you feel different, I don't want you to miss out on the greatest love of your life because you made assumptions. Or because you thought you might get hurt again. It would be easy for you to give up and walk away. You wouldn't have to face any of your feelings. If there's one thing

I've learned in all my years on this earth, it's that everything turns out as it should," Mrs. Walker said, reclining in her chair.

"Thank you," Mrs. Walker, Viola said. She stood up. She was going to try and put everything out of her mind for now. She would order takeout, put on her pajamas, bake, and curl up with some Christmas movies. She tried to keep Mrs. Walker's words on repeat in her mind: Everything will turn out as it should.

Charlie

Charlie closed the car door, inhaled deeply, and exhaled slowly. If Holly had shown up at his apartment right as he arrived, then maybe he would have taken her back. But he wasn't the same Charlie who had been in love with Holly. Viola was a part of him whether he wanted her to be or not. Maybe she was always there, and he just needed to uncover her.

Before pulling off from the airport line, he sent a text to Viola:

Can we talk?

He put the directions back to the apartment in his GPS and hoped she would respond by the time he got there. He could always just knock on her door. Either way, he didn't want to wait another second.

The roads were pretty congested, and he wondered if traffic was always like this.

It wasn't quite as bad as New York, but it was pretty horrible. It felt like an eternity before he was pulling into the parking lot of his apartment building. He checked his phone as soon as he stopped the car.

No response from Viola.

Should he give her some space, or should he just go straight to her? He knew he should probably wait to hear back from her, but he didn't want to wait. He didn't quite understand why, but it felt pressing that he tell her exactly how he felt. He quickened his pace and made his way to the front of the building. His heart was doing double time, both from the brisk walking and from the nervous energy electrifying his insides.

Once he arrived in front of her door, he raised his hand to knock, but stopped when he realized it would have resulted in a bang if he had knocked with the force he intended to. Instead, he dropped his arm and let out a deep breath to re-center. He lifted his hand once again, and this time brought it lightly to the door. He didn't hear anything at first, and then there was rustling.

Good, she was home.

After a few seconds, the door swung open, and there was Viola. Her curls were piled in a messy bun, and she wore Christmas tree pajamas. She could have been all dressed up with makeup and a fancy dress but still wouldn't be as beautiful as she was in this moment. She was stunning when she dressed up, but her most natural state was spellbinding. All he wanted to do was pull her close.

"Um," Viola said, staring at him with equal bewilderment. "Did you want to come inside?"

He almost forgot how to speak. At last, he said, "Yeah," and swallowed. It was all he could manage to get out.

Viola's apartment was warm and inviting. She had a Christmas tree in the corner with white lights and red and gold ornaments. It was next to a large desk with colorful markers, pens, pencils, and various kinds of paper in neat piles. He inhaled and closed his eyes for a second. Something sweet was in the oven.

"Are you baking cookies? he asked.

"Homemade Christmas donuts," she said. She smiled, but it wasn't a real smile.

A tiny ache tugged at his heart, knowing he was likely responsible.

"Smells wonderful."

"I thought you'd be off somewhere with Holly," Viola said. Now her smile had totally disappeared, her expression a fortress.

"I have something I need to say, Viola."

Viola

Viola almost couldn't believe he was standing in the middle of her living room. Since he walked in, the two of them hadn't moved much, both of them too tense to take a seat.

"I, uh, bought some extra lights and decorations for The Center on my way back home," he said.

Normally, she'd be melting over a gesture like that, but it was hard to get excited right now.

"What do you want, Charlie? That can't be the only reason you wanted to talk," Viola said, cutting straight to the point. She might as well.

"I guess I could see why you'd think I'd be off with Holly, but I don't think you understand," Charlie said.

"There's not much to understand," she

said, looking him straight in the eyes.

"That's what I'm trying to tell you. I didn't get back together with Holly. I just gave her a ride to the airport—back to New York," he said, the corners of his mouth turning up a bit.

The tempo of her heart accelerated. "What?" she asked. Her thoughts sprinted off with no direction. Every thought, every scenario that she had played in her mind swirled in a continuous fog. "You're not taking her back?"

"I'm sure that's what Holly would want. But I can't do it. I'm not her version of Charlie anymore. Things change," he said.

"Is that so?" Violet said. She couldn't help but smile.

"That's so." Charlie took a step towards her. "I came racing back to tell you that I couldn't wait a moment longer. All I want is more slow dancing with you to Christmas songs and more Christmas donuts… and more Christmases," he said, his smile growing wider.

"Me?" Viola said. The energy in the room was electric, and everything in it—

especially Charlie—lit her up.

"Yeah, *you*," he said, reaching into his pocket. "Why is it so hard for you to believe that you're transcendent? You are wonder and sunlight, and you take my breath away every time I'm near you." He pulled out the red envelope.

Viola squinted as he held it in his hand.

"When you left the taco place that first evening we had dinner, you left this," he said, unfolding the piece of paper and holding it up. The light from the Christmas tree made it glow.

"My letter—you've had it this whole time?"

He took another step closer. "Haven't you noticed I've been making every attempt to check all your boxes? I read your letter, and I just wanted to make you happy this Christmas. I ended up making myself happy too," he said.

"I had no idea where I dropped it. I was actually worried you found it and would think I was nuts," she said, laughing. She took the letter in her hands and read over it. "I forgot I wrote all those things." She smiled as all the memories of their outings came flooding back. The dancing, the donuts, the Christmas lights stroll. "I—I don't know what to say," she said, looking up from the letter and meeting Charlie's gaze.

"I know we didn't meet too long ago, but I gotta tell you. Checking your boxes is a job I wouldn't mind having for the rest of my life," he said.

"You can't possibly know—"

"I know. We don't have to get married tomorrow, Viola, but I *know*."

"No one has ever done anything like that for me—or made me feel this way," she said, trying not to cry.

"So do you think we can see where this goes—maybe have more donuts with me?" he asked.

Viola nodded, her lips stretching into a gleaming smile. This time she took a step closer to Charlie, the space between them shrinking.

Charlie wrapped an arm around her waist and drew her in until there wasn't any space left.

Every inch of her skin charged with electricity. She was high voltage, and it was because of Charlie. She couldn't take her eyes off him as he tilted his head down, and she reached up. Once their lips connected, every beat of her heart felt like a revolution. No one else would ever do.

She pulled away and stared into his warm brown eyes. They made her want to come in from the cold.

"Did Santa grant your Christmas wish?" Charlie asked.

"I think he *over* delivered," Viola said, tracing his jawline.

"Merry Christmas, Viola."

"Merry Christmas, Charlie."

I love hearing from my readers and seeing photos of them enjoying my books online! Tag me in your photos on Instagram, Twitter, and Facebook: @racquelhenry!

You can also stay up-to-date on new releases and writing news via my newsletter: racquelhenry.com/newsletter.

Also by *Racquel Henry*

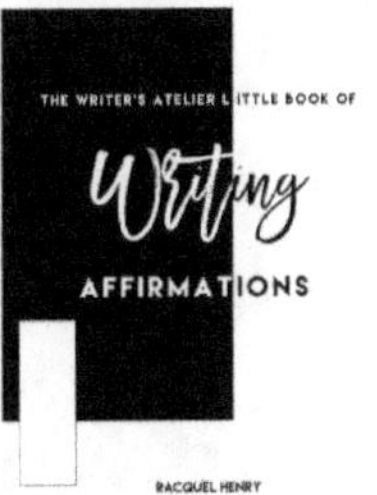

Find out more about Racquel and sign up for her newsletter at
www.racquelhenry.com

Find more publications at
https://racquelhenry.com/publications/